PRETEND YOU LOVE ME

W. WINTERS
AMELIA WILDE

PRETEND YOU LOVE ME

W Winters and Amelia Wilde

All I have to do is pretend. When the lights go out and the chill of the cell creeps in, I know I must go along with everything he says.

His sharp gaze fades into the darkness, and nothing else matters but surviving this moment.

I'll do all he asks. I'll obey every command and submit on my knees. There's not an ounce of me that's willing to risk losing more than I already have.

All he desired was revenge, and now all he desires is me.

This mafia story is an explicit abduction romance with violence and dubious consent. It's short and provocative, with a jaw-dropping twist. The tale's decadent darkness allows us to escape into the fantasy. Please be mindful of these triggers prior to reading.

PROLOGUE

The front door creaks open ever so slowly and softly. The faint sound is immediately drowned out by the loud music, the laughter and the clink of chips falling onto the poker table in the back room. The space is filled with cigar smoke and brutal men whose faces hold genuine smiles as they gamble with stolen money. A half dozen of them are tucked away in the back of the modern home.

Seven men filter in through the front, dressed all in black, with leather gloves but no masks.

In that very front room there's a crib and next to it a lullaby sound machine on the fireplace mantel, meant to lull the infant into a sweet dream. Chubby little hands wrap around a rattle as wide eyes watch but can't see that far as the men take careful steps through the hall.

The floor groans in protest, but just like the front door, it's unheard. Not a single one of them expected anything more than drinking and betting during their monthly poker game.

The song's soothing refrain is punctuated by the staccato bang of guns cutting through the night. Feminine steps race down the stairs at the front of the home, rushing with the silent terror of a mother. Her screams are joined by shouting. Chaos only lasts a moment, one blur, one execution carried out seamlessly and planned for years.

The lullaby never stops as one of the assailants grabs the woman by her waist. The baby can't see how she struggles in the unknown man's arms to reach her child. She pleads and prays but can't do anything other than thrash in the arms of someone more prepared, and far stronger than she.

The sweet melody is at such odds with the silence that follows a bullet pinging on the tiled floor. Bodies lie around the poker table, blood seeping into the sides of tailored suits and what were once crisp white button-downs.

It's quiet, all but the cadence of a lullaby the infant has heard since before he was born. Footsteps aren't so careful anymore as the music suddenly halts and the men filter out. The woman is carried away, all the while fighting for her child.

One man approaches the crib, and two rough, callused hands wrap around the top railing. A bundled baby, wrapped tightly yet those little arms somehow escaped, looks up at dark eyes.

A gruff voice whispers something to the man who stares down at the child, and he only gives a nod in response. He's murdered more men than he's shaken hands with.

The man carefully picks up the child, bringing the one-month-old to his chest. "Hush now, little one."

Madelyn

My breathing hardly comes in as another scream tears through my throat. Tears prick my eyes, burning them as I slam my fists against the trunk.

I've been taken, I'm trapped and nothing is in

my control anymore. A terror that threatens to consume me takes over.

"My baby!" I cry out again, pleading with men who ignore me. "Please!" I beg them.

They won't listen, though. Even as panic tenses all my body, and adrenaline pounds through my veins, I'm all too aware they won't listen to me.

I know what he wants. My racing heart slows.

A chill settles through me as I hear a knock on the steel roof above me. "You be quiet now, you don't want to wake the baby," a man says, his voice carrying through the metal enclosure of the trunk.

"Please," I whisper so lowly, I'm not certain a soul could hear.

The command comes out final yet tinged with sympathy, although I may be wrong. Perhaps I only imagine a semblance of mercy. "You listen to me, and everything will be all right."

Connor
Two days ago

My brother's footsteps crunch in the snow. Fletcher's silent, but I'm more than certain I know what he plans to say. A bitter wind whips by, my black tie waving in the breeze as I stare down at the carved stones in the ground. Two people who should have never been laid to rest will lie here for all eternity.

"What is it?" I barely manage to ask after I swallow the hard lump in my throat. It's all for them, for my wife and son I lost years ago, yet it feels like I've betrayed them.

"Is there anything I can do?" my brother questions behind me and it's so softly spoken, the harsh wind nearly drowns out the words.

Turning to face him, his hands are splayed across the front of his charcoal suit. Remorse wears itself on his face whenever we find ourselves here.

"It's been six years," I say, telling him a truth he already knows.

He only nods and then clears his throat as he takes the necessary steps to close the distance between us. He swallows so hard it's audible before he says, "Friday night, it's set."

With my brother in front of me and my past behind me, I'm all too aware that what I'm going to do next is cruel and unforgivable. He took my wife and child … this is a fair trade.

"Are you sure about this?" he asks.

I don't answer him; all I know is that I need this to happen. More than I need to live.

MADELYN

*T*he trembling is constant and I couldn't stop it if I tried. Another shudder runs through me as the chill of the cell slips across my barely covered skin. My shoulders shake involuntarily as I bring my knees into my chest and stare at the vent where soft promises filter through of what awaits me. I can hear all the men, everything they're saying and how they're to leave me alone.

He said no one touches her.

Leave her there until he's ready.

They don't ask questions but they know I'm here, tucked away in the basement, huddled in a corner of my cell.

There's a soft drip from the spout in the cinder block wall behind me that's a relative constant and occasionally the heat kicks on, a loud click signaling its start but the warmth isn't for the cell, it's for upstairs.

The cotton nightgown I was wearing when I was taken is torn and thin, leaving me freezing, alone and waiting for the same person as the men upstairs: Connor Walsh.

Just thinking his name does horrid things to my heart. It skips and halts in place. The rough stubble of his jaw, the hard lines of his cheekbones and the depths of his dark copper gaze only add to the dominating air that surrounds him.

He's a damaged man with nothing left to lose. Men like him are dangerous. That's what my husband used to say. He knew that all too well and now he's dead.

Leaving my fate in the hands of a man hell-bent on revenge.

The unmistakable sound of a key turning in the lock from up the stairwell sends a pulse of shock and a new wave of terror through me. The first step on the narrow wooden stairs seems hesitant, as if whoever owns the movement is unsure of it. With my palms scraping against the grit littering the floor I attempt to scoot backward, as far away as I can get, but the stone wall at my back is unyielding.

Step by step, he takes his time.

His black jeans come into view first, followed by his black button-down with the sleeves rolled up to his forearms. The shirt is tight on his broad shoulders, and then those eyes … they pin me where I am.

Connor is a hardened man; I've known him nearly all my life. Or at least I've known the whispers of him. In this small run-down town with corruption on every corner, two feuding families ran things for decades. There was my husband's family, the mob formed by his father, and there were the Walshes.

Now there's only Connor Walsh.

His heavy footsteps stop outside the barred door of the cell. The room I'm confined to feels so much like a prison, for a moment I think of Connor as my warden.

The tension is thick between us and even though he's feet away, I'm enveloped by his heat.

The cords in his neck tighten as he swallows, his gaze roaming down my body, appraising every inch as it travels lower.

Too much time passes in near silence and fear takes over, begging me to plead with him. "My baby—"

"You'll do what I say." His tone is low and his words spoken with a cadence that's calm and eerie. It's one I've never heard from him. One that paralyzes me. "Did you hear me?" he questions and tilts his head, as if willing me to defy him.

Something I have no intention of doing.

"Anything. I'll do anything you tell me to," I say, the words leaving me in a rush.

"Good."

"My baby?" I'm barely able to get the words out. He's only a month old. My little one.

"He's fine." He has the decency to pull his eyes away from me as he speaks. "He's taken care of, and you'll be with him soon."

Hope rises along with an eagerness to get to my baby.

"Come here," Connor commands and I don't hesitate. Unsure of whether I should stand or crawl, I crawl, lifting the torn nightgown and balling the fabric in my fists. The floor isn't gentle on my knuckles but I don't care.

It's not until I get to the bars that he tells me, "You could have walked."

Embarrassment colors my cheeks and just as I look up at him to tell him I don't know what he wants, he reaches through the bars, and his strong fingers wrap around my throat.

Instinctively my hands reach up to his, and I instantly regret it.

He isn't tight with his grip, just firm, not so much that I feel the need to fight. Slowly, reluctantly, I lower my hands. All the while his amber gaze blazes and keeps me still.

"Stand," he tells me and I do as he wishes.

A chill filters through and my nipples harden; the thin gown does nothing to hide that fact. Staring down at the veins in his arms, I attempt to hide the shame of what comes over me.

"You know what I want from you, don't you?" he questions, his breath low and not hiding his desire.

I attempt to nod without looking up at him, but his grip tightens and my eyes flash to his.

"Yes," I answer in a whisper.

My heart pounds as heat floods through me with the way he looks at me. It's the same way he looked at me years ago, before the war, before the bloodshed, before he became the man he is today. Years ago when we were reckless and life hadn't taught us how harsh it could be.

His hand loosens just enough for his thumb to

brush along my bottom lip, prompting me to open my mouth.

"Suck," he murmurs this time and I do as I'm told. The roughness of his skin begs me to scrape my teeth along it and I do. I suck the taste of him, I press my tongue against him and give him exactly what I know he wants.

It's only when my eyes close that he pulls away, leaving me standing there with the bars between us and a power imbalance that puts me at his mercy.

He reaches into his pocket for the key, and plays with it between his thumb and pointer, as if debating.

My pulse rampages but before I can beg for anything from this man, he tells me, "Your child needs you. Get him back to sleep, then you'll come to me. Understand?"

CONNOR

*V*oices come through the back door as I move through the house. My brother and three of our men are outside, having a smoke. Their cigarettes are orange flares in the dark. The wood beneath my feet doesn't creak to announce my presence. They don't hear me getting closer to the door.

I pause to listen. At times their voices are muffled by the sound of the vengeful wind. In general, they're not paying attention. The men talk freely among themselves, not bothering to give the surrounding woods more than a cursory glance. It's not the woods they should be worried about.

It's me.

After years of working for me, and knowing

how close to the edge I've been, they should be more than aware of that fact.

Their lack of attention will play into my hands, but it frustrates me just the same. I haven't had the luxury of letting my guard down.

Most people have no guard at all, even the men who are supposed to. They can't keep their mouths shut. A man who can listen is always better off. That's what it takes to survive in the world today. You have to keep track of what's going on around you, even with people you claim to trust.

I don't trust anyone. Least of all the men outside. My brother is the only one who deserves my trust, and he's the only one who will get it. Everyone else is expendable. Everyone else can be replaced in a heartbeat. The vast majority of the world simply takes up space until someone has a better use for it.

I wouldn't have thought that when I was younger. I had softer ideas about the value of human life. Now, I don't give a fuck.

Except when it comes to my new captive and prize.

Madelyn.

Everything in me screams to go back to her. It's unsettling. I shut off my emotions six years ago. It was like flipping the switch to a circuit breaker. Every feeling apart from rage died out in an instant, and I haven't let any of the others come back. It would be impossible to focus with my mind occupied by sentiments and morals.

"What do you make of it?" Fletcher asks the men. They feel secure, out in the backyard. It's a mistake. The cover of darkness isn't a cover at all. Just because they've carried out the mission successfully doesn't mean it's any safer. Loyalty has been questioned recently. I deliberately chose the three newest men, fledgling additions.

If loyalty isn't given freely, I won't demand it. I'll simply cut their throats.

"She'll run the first chance she gets," answers the first one. I recognize the voice as belonging to Matthew. After a long drag of his cigarette he adds, "Had that look in her eyes. She's ready to bolt."

"Not if she cares for her child," my brother points out. I swallow thickly at the reminder of the little boy. Those emotions I thought long dead shove themselves to the surface and I clench my fist in response.

"You think he'll really keep her?" asks the second, Nathaniel. He lights a new cigarette and it casts orange light across his face. "Like he really wants to keep her as his … what? Sex slave?"

"It's sick," Matthew practically spits out. "More than a little."

"Is that the first hint you ever got that my brother's sick?" my brother asks in a light, joking manner, but there's a razor blade at the heart of his tone. I don't have to see him to know there's a smirk on his face. Right now he's seemingly charming and at ease, but it conceals a lethal side of him.

"You think I'm sick?" I say as I stride out into the backyard. They've been in the business too long to look truly surprised, but the first one frowns. He didn't want me to overhear him call me sick. It's a lapse. The third man has been silent and he remains still, his arms crossed as he leans against the brick of the house.

The other two exchange self-conscious glances, like they've been caught with their dicks out.

"She's in a cell, isn't she?" The question is followed by another drag from the first man's cigarette. "After all that screaming."

I'd rather stay cold, but emotions run hot. "She's doing what I told her to do."

He smirks. "How? Doesn't seem like she'll be very cooperative."

"That depends on who handles her. So it's a good thing you assholes won't be touching her."

He huffs a humorless laugh with his hands up. "I'm not the one who wants to. You spent too long in there. People are going to think you want her, and she's not like that."

"Not like what?"

The first man darts a glance at his buddy. This is risky territory, and he knows it. The mood is lightening but my face isn't.

"Worth it," he says. "What happens if she gets to you? What happens if she makes you even sicker than you already are?"

"I'll let you know if I feel ill when I'm done with her." I let a smile spread over my face. That's what he's watching. He doesn't see the quick reach for the gun at my belt. He's too busy laughing.

The safety's been off since we took her. I've been waiting for this moment. Waiting for one of them to step out of line.

Damn it, I wasn't supposed to care. None of the comments were going to get to me. I wasn't going to feel anything for her. Not at the house. Not in the cell. Nowhere.

Not until it was time.

The situation is already getting out of control, but my gun isn't.

I pull the trigger, sending a bullet through his head. Anger surges through my veins. There are things no one can ever know about Madelyn. There are things I'll have to keep buried deep until this is over.

A spatter of blood lands on my cheek as his body drops with a dull thud. I've been at this long enough to recognize the sound of a dead man hitting the ground.

I wait a beat.

Watch him.

No sign of movement comes from the body, except for the blood seeping out of the wound.

I swipe at the blood on my cheek with the back of my hand.

The other men are silent. Cigarettes burn at the tips of their fingers. Not a soul makes a move. The second guy was standing close enough that he has to be bloodied. Impossible to tell for sure with our dark clothes and the dark night. His face is frozen.

"Mind cleaning this up for me, brother?"

Fletcher doesn't appear disturbed in the least by the death of one of the members of our team. His mouth quirks. Not quite a smile. Not quite a frown. More like acceptance. Like he expected this. All of them should have expected this from me. I've been this person for six years now. I'm not going to change because Madelyn is in a cell.

"Not at all, boss."

I adjust my sleeves as my brother steps over to the body. He bends down and feels for a pulse. It's not necessary. The man's dead.

"Did anyone else have any comments about my future wife before I leave?"

I didn't intend to react to what they were saying, but my pounding heart didn't get the memo. *Sick*. I'll be damned. It was a simple bullshit comment that didn't mean anything. I felt it like a bullet through flesh.

The anger I've kept buried for the last six years is alive and well. It doesn't matter that I flipped the switch. It's all come back in an instant.

None of them has a damn thing to say. The only thing that surrounds us is silence and the threat of imminent death if they dare to say another word.

The third man taps the ash off his cigarette. He backs up half a step from the body, leaving room for my brother to roll the dead man onto his back.

"Get the wheelbarrow," my brother orders.

Everyone snaps into motion. They'll need to dig a hole at the edge of the woods, tip the body into it, and cover him back up. Not a single word is spoken in protest. Now that I've made my point, we shouldn't have any further conflict.

I've been patient. I've been meticulous. I've been planning.

Now that I have her, I'm going to use her to my advantage and use her for my pleasure.

If that makes me sick, so be it. It's time to enjoy the spoils of revenge.

MADELYN

*W*ith his hand on my shoulder and
his rough heated skin against
mine, he opens the bedroom door.

The baby is sleeping. Soundly and at a distance
where I'll hear if he wakes.

This is the price I'll pay for the life I lead and
the desires I've had for as long as I've known what
it means to exist in this world.

A fire is already lit, surrounded by a stone
mantel that reaches to the ceiling. The simplicity
and masculinity of the room are undeniable. A gray
textured wallpaper lines the back wall, while
woodsy tones paired with blacks and grays add to
the dominating atmosphere. The massive bed is a

king and at the end of it is a tufted warm brown
leather ottoman.

I've always seen Connor as a rugged man.
Ruthless and foreboding. I never could have imagined his private room to have such warmth and
elegance. The harsh lines and darkness certainly fit
his persona, though.

With a heavy breath, I peek down at myself and
my arms instinctively cover my chest. The torn
cotton gown appears cheap and out of place in a
space like this. My knees are dirty and although the
room itself is warm and expensive, all I feel is cold
and trapped.

"This needs to come off," Connor whispers
behind me, his warm breath just beneath the shell of
my ear. His light touch on my bare shoulders as he
brushes down the straps of my nightgown causes
me to shiver involuntarily. A line of goosebumps
travels down my curves as the nightgown falls. It
doesn't do so elegantly, as silk would have. As it
catches at my wide hips, Connor uses both hands to
push the garment down and his thumbs hook my
underwear, tugging it along with the fabric.

Completely bared, my nipples pebble and I
struggle to inhale as I stare straight ahead at the
roaring fire. The flames lick and hiss while Connor

takes his time, barely touching me, but exposing me exactly how he wishes.

My body isn't what it used to be and as his hand splays against my stomach, my eyes close with worry, but his hum of satisfaction spreads a new sensation through me. He nips the lobe of my ear and a gasp is forced from me.

As my breathing picks up, his hand lowers and his chest hits my back.

His fingers slip down to my sensitive clit. He takes his time, toying with me until my body buckles forward. His forearm braces me against him and he tsks.

"You'll stay still as I play with you," he tells me, his tone holding a note of warning. His hardened length presses into my backside through his jeans. His hard body demands that I take it.

My hand, though, acts on its own accordingly, grabbing his wrist as his hand moves lower still to my slit.

His body stills and the air changes. I can barely breathe knowing what I've done. I've stopped him, I've deliberately disobeyed.

"I haven't—" I start to say but can barely speak. "Since the baby," I add, pushing out the excuse. I haven't touched myself or been touched.

My chest rises and falls chaotically, uncertain how he'll react.

All at once, he leaves me, and I only turn when the sound of the sheets and comforter being lifted is louder than my pulse racing in my ears.

In the near silent room, all I can think about is my now dead husband's cruelty. Random flashes greet me of every time my needs were denied. Memories drift into my mind of my brother and how he died needlessly. Every dark moment passes in the flick of a second. My throat closes and the strength I thought I had fades to nothing but a facade.

I watch the dark shadows play along Connor's body as he pulls his shirt over his head, dropping it to the floor to form a puddle of clothing. His hands move to his belt and it comes off nearly violently to the point where I'm tempted to take a step back. He drops it, though, and it lands with a heavy thud. His jeans are next, and in one swift motion his cock juts out.

In only a moment, the damaged man is completely bared to me and waiting.

"Get on the bed," Connor commands and my body moves immediately, instantly obeying. Everything in me is at war; every want, every need, every thought and memory.

The bed groans softly as I climb onto the center and lie down on the luxurious sheets. My head sinks into the pillow and my gaze finds the spinning fan.

He's deliberate as he crawls up the bed, but his touch still startles me and brings me back to the present when he asks, "Is there something on your mind?"

My answer is immediate and submissive. "What would you like to be on my mind?"

Sliding between my legs, he spreads my thighs and his hard body covers me. His warm skin presses against my chest and he caresses my curves. His mouth greets me, his lips molding to mine instantly as his tongue parts my seam.

It's been so long since I've been kissed like *this*. Heavily and wantonly. Since I've been moaned into by the mouth of a man. His tongue strokes against mine as his fingers press into the flesh of my hips and he keeps me pinned. It feels as if he's everywhere all at once.

Consuming me and demanding attention equally as much as desire.

When he breaks the kiss, I breathlessly stare back at him, transfixed by his copper gaze.

"You will think of nothing but this. Of how much you need me to take you."

The light of the fire displays the harshness of his collarbone and corded muscles as I part my lips to answer. I can't, though, because he's far too concerned with silencing me with another kiss.

It's demanding and brutal, but the gentle motion of his hand slipping between my thighs is very much at odds. He's focused on my clit until I writhe under him, unable to stay still as he told me I should.

Every nerve ending lights on fire, a bundle explodes in the pit of my stomach and I cry out my pleasure as an orgasm rocks through my body. It happens so quickly and so unexpectedly, smothering every thought and doubt along with it.

He's off of me the moment I've come, and it doesn't take me long to figure out why. From his nightstand he gathers a bottle, and I watch him stroke himself with lubrication before pouring more in his hands.

It's only then that his fingers slip lower once again, spreading the lube at my entrance.

On his knees between my thighs, he slips the

head of his cock between my folds, toying with me before pressing in slightly. My breath hitches and my hand splays against his chest as if that could stop him. With his dark gaze focused on mine, he tells me in a murmur, "I will ruin you for everyone else, but I intend for you to enjoy every moment."

With that he presses in deeper, stretching me and making my lips form an *O*. The sensation stings for a moment until he's fully inside of me, pressing against my walls. Connor stills, allowing me time to adjust.

My blunt nails dig into his shoulders as I wrap my arms around him, the heels of my feet digging into his muscular ass, as if I could hold on. As if doing so will save me from the far too intense sensation.

As I stare above me wide eyed and attempting to breathe, he kisses and nips my neck, relaxing me slowly as he pulls out gently and presses back in.

His lips find mine again and I'm able to kiss him, to cling to him, grateful and relieved. My body heats with every small movement. Every rock of his hips causes him to brush against my clit and it isn't long before I tilt my hips, wanting him deeper.

The moment my body instinctively welcomes

him, he smiles against my lips. "You're my good little whore, aren't you?"

At his question my eyes meet his and he slams inside of me, brutally.

My head falls back and a strangled moan leaves me.

"Your cunt was made for me to fuck," he tells me as his hips piston.

His body pins me and his left hand finds my neck. Fingers wrap tight around my throat as he pounds into me, relentlessly and bringing about an intense sensation I've never felt before.

The bed bows with every hard thrust.

"Come on my cock like you want to," he groans into the crook of my neck. My pebbled nipples brush against his chest and it's all too much. "Come for me, my good little whore."

I do it. Unashamedly, I come undone for him.

The moan of satisfaction only extends my pleasure.

The orgasm is still raging through me as he kisses me again, riding through my release and fucking me deeper and harder. "That's my good girl. You're so fucking perfect."

He doesn't finish like that. He turns me over onto my stomach, grabbing the base of my hair and tugging as he fucks me from behind, dragging out every orgasm and pausing before he reaches his own climax so he can take more time with me.

"I'm going to enjoy every inch of you. I'm going to make you completely mine."

CONNOR

She's terrified with the men watching.

At least that's how it looks from my perspective. Her previously timid glances have turned to wide-eyed stares. Her chest rises and falls rapidly. Are these real nerves or is she pretending? Or is she just feeling the effects of what we did together?

Fuck knows I am. She's perfect. I already knew she would be. But last night was fucking perfect.

When she's cleaned up, presentable as she can be given the circumstances, I bring her out to the kitchen. She barely slept. All she wears is my T-shirt and an oversized pair of pajama pants rolled up at her hips.

Her hair is combed through but her fragility and delicate features are entirely exposed. For a split second I question my pride given her fear. But she's fucking perfect and she's mine. All mine. Forever.

She is the only good to come from chaos and war. How could I not be obsessed with her?

With hesitant steps, I have to press against the small of her back to bring her to the kitchen. It's modern, much like the entire estate, with clean lines and granite and stone that touch nearly every surface. I imagine she'll change it. As far as I'm concerned, it's hers to do as she wishes and needs.

Her delicate hand forms a fist, balling up the fabric of my shirt as we enter the room. Her bare feet pad softly, almost silently, on the cold tiled floor.

The men have arranged themselves there around the table. None of them appear to have slept last night. There's always the risk of retribution. No one will be safe or secure for weeks, months, maybe even longer. Not until the last enemy is snuffed out.

My brother watches Madelyn and I get closer without so much as a glimmer of recognition in his eyes. Best for everyone that way. He's the only one who knows her. He's the only one who knows the whole story. And it'll stay that way.

"Madelyn, this is my brother." I bring her over to him first. She's shaking like a leaf as he holds his hand out for her to shake.

"Hello, Madelyn," he says easily with the charming air he's known for. Although he's kind, she's still hesitant and looks to me first before she takes his hand.

"Hi," she says. I can hardly hear the words as they make small talk.

Madelyn lets me introduce her to all the men. She's a good actress. She's known who these men are for years. Knows their faces.

And they know her. They know far too much.

I don't care for the way they look at her, gazing too long and appraising. My hand itches to clench a fist, to express my rage for their indecency. I don't. I have to pretend I don't feel the anger surging inside every time one of them looks down at her body instead of her face. I have to pretend that there's nothing behind this but revenge.

That she's my captive, that this was planned in the way they're aware. That we haven't used them and there weren't ulterior motives.

The sound of the baby crying drifts into the kitchen. It's soft. He has the calmest cry.

Madelyn reacts instantly, her body tensing up as she looks over her shoulder, toward the hallway to her child. She bites at her lip but doesn't take a step toward the sound.

"Go," I tell her.

She hesitates, those wide eyes peeking up at me.

"Are you going to make me repeat myself?" I question lowly with a hint of playfulness, although she doesn't let on that she registers it.

Her eyes meet mine, and I swear I can see real fear there. *Of them? Of me?* I have to admit I like the look of it in her eyes. If that makes me sick, then so be it.

I take her jaw between my thumb and forefinger and tug her lips toward mine. I have to pretend I don't enjoy it. That it's part of the job. But it feels damn good to have my fingers on her skin. Her pulse is right at the surface. Her heart is beating hard, and something else flashes into her eyes. Desire. She can't hide it from me, no matter how well she pretends with the other men.

It's a good thing I have practice in following the plan. I want to drag her back to my bedroom, but this little performance is important for what happens next. The men need to see us together. They need to see me controlling her and her submission. There can be no question about what's happening between me and Madelyn.

Revenge. Ownership.

Nothing else. There is only one truth now: she is mine.

"What did I tell you?"

Madelyn parts her lips. "That I'll do what you say."

I want to say that she needs to do more. That she needs to kiss me, right here, right now. Make me believe it. But that would end my ability to speak, and I have more to say. The baby cries out again. He sounds more desperate now. Hungry or lonely, it's hard to tell. I don't let on that I'm responding to the noise too. A man like me shouldn't ever want to comfort a crying child. Certainly not one that everyone believes is another man's child.

"What else?" I ask her. "What else did I tell you? There are only two things that matter. You will do what I say … and what else?"

"That I'm yours." *I'm yours* sounds sweet on her tongue. It doesn't matter that we're in a room full of killers. It doesn't matter that I'm the most dangerous one of all.

"Do you think what's mine hesitates in my own home?"

Madelyn shakes her head, pressing her face more firmly into my hand.

It's going to be hell to let go of her. I keep thinking I can make this easy. I've endured many difficult things over the years. Staying in control is my entire life. I even planned this operation from start to finish. Everything about it was my doing. This should have been the simple part—pretending she's just a captive who will marry me against her will.

"You're a mother. And you're my fuck toy. You'll marry me and love me in every way I crave." I say these words in a cruel, mocking tone that's meant to hurt her, but they're true. They're the only real thing about this situation. Madelyn will marry me. She'll stay my fuck toy. And she is a mother.

The baby cries again, and my fingers tighten in spite of all my control. It's a sound designed to attract attention, but I can't give in. I can't be the one to scoop the child from the crib and give it whatever comfort it needs. Not with the eyes of my men on me.

"Don't you love me?" I say in a taunting tone.

Madelyn flinches, and once again, I'm flooded

with confusion. Is she flinching because she doesn't believe me or because she's afraid of reality? Now is not the time for that conversation, but damn, I wish it were.

"I love you," she says, her voice soft.

I pull her in for a brutal kiss.

This—this is the thing I can't stop. I meant for it to be quick, but once her mouth is against mine, I'm consumed with how sweet she is. She doesn't pull away from the harsh bite. Instead, she gives into it. She's obedient that way, but it only makes me want to keep her here with me.

It's a dangerous line we're walking.

Until we follow this situation to the end, everything will be as uncertain as it is now. Anything could happen. That's one thing this life has taught me. It's not over just because you want something to be done. It's over when the last threat is finally defeated.

We're not there yet. Not even close.

I pull away from her, and Madelyn stumbles. It takes all my willpower not to pull her into my arms and steady her. She catches herself before I have to and straightens slowly, her breath coming fast.

"Now go," I order.

The baby wails now, sustained cries. I can see

the physical pull he has on her. Maybe it's similar to the pull she has on me.

Once Madelyn has her balance, she leaves quickly, not glancing back at any of us.

Not surprising. She doesn't want the other men to look at her. It was hard enough for her to be in the kitchen with all of them. Still, I would have felt some satisfaction if she'd looked back for me.

It doesn't matter. I'm the one who ordered her to go. That doesn't include hesitating to see if I'm watching. I made that clear enough when I spoke to her. I can still feel her warm flesh pressing against my fingers when she shook her head. It's unreal, how this woman gets under my skin. I almost wipe my palm against my pants just to get the sensation to go away. I can't let it influence me.

I can't bring myself to do it. The tingling where our bodies touched lingers on my hand.

I want to follow her more than anything. Instead, I imagine her entering the baby's room, her body relaxing as she sees her child again. She's a good mother, and she would soften. Murmur something to him as she came in so he'd know she was there.

I was right. The cries taper off. She must have him in her arms now, holding him close.

If we were different people, I'd be in there with her. I feel more regret about that than I should. Having feelings like this is almost overwhelming, given how hard I've worked to keep them suppressed over the years.

It doesn't matter. I won't let them interfere. Madelyn and I will get to the end of this, whether it goes as planned or blows up in our faces.

I turn back to the men gathered at the table. If they noticed anything different about the way I treated her, they don't give any sign of it. That's a relief.

"Time to move on," I tell them. "Any movement or word? Has anyone heard anything?"

MADELYN

 e fills me with every thrust. Each motion is forceful and brutal, yet it all brings nothing but pleasure. With a pillow under my hips, he fucks me deep and rough. A cold sweat breaks out along my skin. I'm sore, deliciously used and my entire being is exhausted and sated.

As he buries himself fully inside of me, his hand roughly plucks my nipples and his pubic hair grinds against my clit. He's an expert at playing me, at depriving me of pleasure until he's ready.

It's been that way for years now, and the memory of our first time against the brick wall of an alley flashes before my eyes as he tells me to come like the good little whore I am.

Just like he did then.

And I obey, dutifully coming undone for a man I've loved in secret for years.

As he loses himself to pleasure, the rhythmic pulses of his cock press against my walls and I swear I could come again just from the sensation.

He holds me, kisses me for a moment and then climbs off, leaving me waiting for a damp cloth to clean up. He's gentle as he does it. I've always been in awe of how this man can be so cruel and so hell-bent on murder and vengeance, yet in the dark of night, alone with me, he has a side to him no one else sees.

Although I suppose it's the same for me. I'm a duplicitous woman who married a man only to get back at him for my brother's murder.

The bed groans as he wipes between my thighs and the cuffs attached to the bedpost clink.

"Do you want to use these?" I ask, only because they've been there since I arrived and he hasn't once mentioned them.

"No, it's for if they come in," he states simply, even though dread consumes me.

No one can know I was a rat. No one can know we planned this for years. So much is in the hands of deceit. "You'll say I put them on you at night," he tells me, tossing the cloth into the laundry bin and then climbing back into bed, pulling the sheets and comforter over us.

I can only nod as words evade me. I don't know what all his men think or what they're telling one another. I don't know if I'm playing the part well enough.

My whispered words are laced with fear when I ask, "Do you think they'll find out?"

"My brother knows and no one else. No one can ever suspect you were a rat, even if I told you exactly what to do. They would never trust you."

"I know, but have they said anything?" I ask him as I turn onto my side, staring into the eyes of a man I fell in love with before I was even on his radar. Years ago, before my brother died and I vanished. Before he met a woman who gave him his first son.

Before tragedy. Before this life requested we pay our dues.

Back when all I wanted was him and I thought that would be easy.

"You're giving me that look again." Connor breaks up my thoughts with a gentle murmur, his fingers tipping my chin up and forcing me to look at him.

My handsome brutal protector peers down at me.

"I know I used you. I know you fell for me before I fell for you."

"I loved you so much, I was willing to marry the enemy." My heart aches knowing what I've done.

"You wanted vengeance too," he reminds me and I nod in agreement. I wanted to kill him, but Connor convinced me to destroy them all. Every last one of them from the inside out.

"When did you want me?"

"Always." His answer is easy and confident, without hesitation. "When did I fall in love with you, though? When did I … feel this possessiveness over you?"

"Was it when I got pregnant?" I ask him the question I've wondered for the last nearly year. Everything changed when I told Connor I was pregnant.

"Before that." He admits, "I couldn't stand the idea of him touching you." I remember the argument we had. Connor didn't want me to go back. But we were so close to having our plans realized, and I wanted vengeance more than I cared to protect myself.

"He could have found out the baby wasn't his."

"We were careful …" I start and all the thoughts and worries race through my mind. "If Nolan wasn't yours—"

"He's mine." His answer is final. "That is all that matters. No one will ever hurt him."

My throat closes, wanting nothing else than for my son to be safe. With the feud between families ended by bloodshed, he should be safe.

"I will do anything to keep him safe."

"What if they find out?" It is my only worry. The only thing that keeps me from sleeping peacefully now.

"Fletcher and I would kill them all before we let anything happen to you or our son."

The anxiousness doesn't leave me. "I just want it all to be over," I whisper, my gaze falling to his chest.

His hand wraps around mine and he brings my knuckles to his lips, planting a kiss there before telling me, "I asked too much of you." The remorse and regret are evident in his tone.

"What's done is done."

That's what we've said for years as we fell deeper into each other's arms and more and more consumed with plotting an execution to right the sins of the past.

I'm only grateful I'll no longer be sleeping with the enemy.

"You did everything I told you to. You are my good girl." He kisses my forehead and the pride and comfort that come with his praise nearly lull me to sleep.

"I love you. Not only for what you do for me, but because I know you. I know all of you."

His hand slips down my curves when he tells me he loves me too.

"You didn't answer my question, though … When did you fall for me?" I don't know why I need to know so badly. But I do.

"Around the time I told you we were pregnant?" I guess.

"I loved you before that … you know that."

"I know, I just—" I have to steady my breathing before I can get out this pain that radiates inside of me. "But when you … when you wanted to stop it all … when you wanted me to run away from him and be with you because I was pregnant … I was afraid to tell you because I knew you didn't feel for me what I felt for you but something seemed different that day."

He smiles weakly and stares at the spinning fan as he says, "I'll never forget that day."

Before I can press him again, wanting to know when, he tells me, "I fell for you when you came to me with a proposition. It was slow, not all at once. When you told me you knew how I felt." His words are choked and I remember that moment. When I met him at his wife and child's gravestones. My dead husband took from us a love that will always be missed. But Connor and I found each other and he won't take that away now.

He pulls me in close. "I fell in love with you when my soul realized I needed you to exist. I don't know how else to describe it. Without you, I didn't want to live."

Silence surrounds us as I realize the depth of our connection.

"It's our secret, though," he reminds me.

"I know."

His voice is reassuring when he tells me, "You'll do well playing the part, you have before."

"I'll pretend as long as you want, whatever you want. So long as you love me."

His grip on me tightens and he pulls me in as close as I could possibly be. He's my savior, though everyone else thinks he's my enemy. I can only hope I'm the same to him.

"Tell me you love me again," I whisper against his lips.

"I love you."

"I love you too."

Read Willow's sexiest and most talked about
romances in the Merciless World

Ruthless, crime family leader **Carter Cross** should've known Aria would ruin him the moment he saw her. Given to Carter to start a war; he was too eager to accept. But what he didn't know was what Aria would do to him. He didn't know that she would change everything.

Start with Merciless

ALSO BY W. WINTERS

Read Willow's sexiest and most talked about
romances in the Merciless World

This Love Hurts Trilogy
This Love Hurts
But I Need You
And I Love You the Most

An epic tale of both betrayal and all-consuming
love...
Marcus, the villain.
Cody Walsh, the FBI agent who knows too much.
And Delilah, the lawyer caught in between.

What I Would do for You (This Love Hurts Trilogy
Collection)

A Kiss to Tell (a standalone novel)
They lived on the same street and went to the same
school, although he was a year ahead. Even so
close, he was untouchable.
Sebastian was bad news and Chloe was the sad girl
who didn't belong.
Then one night changed everything.

Possessive (a standalone novel)
It was never love with **Daniel Cross** and she never
thought it would be. It was only lust from a
distance. Unrequited love maybe.
He's a man Addison could never have, for so many
reasons.

Merciless Saga
Merciless
Heartless
Breathless
Endless

Ruthless, crime family leader **Carter Cross**
should've known Aria would ruin him the moment

he saw her. Given to Carter to start a war; he was too eager to accept. But what he didn't know was what Aria would do to him. He didn't know that she would change everything.

All He'll Ever Be (Merciless Series Collection of all 4 novels)

Irresistible Attraction Trilogy
A Single Glance
A Single Kiss
A Single Touch

Bethany is looking for answers and to find them she needs one of the brothers of an infamous crime family, **Jase Cross**.
Even a sizzling love affair won't stop her from getting what she needs.
But Bethany soon comes to realise Jase will be her downfall, and she's determined to be his just the same.

Irresistible Attraction (A Single Glance Trilogy Collection)

Hard to Love Series

Hard to Love
Desperate to Touch
Tempted to Kiss
Easy to Fall

Eight years ago she ran from him.
Laura should have known he'd come for her. Men
like **Seth King** always get what they want.
Laura knows what Seth wants from her, and she
knows it comes with a steep price.
However it's a risk both of them will take.

Not My Heart to Break (Hard to Love Series
Collection)

Tease Me Once
Tease me once... I'll kiss you twice.
Declan Cross' story from the Merciless World.

Spin off of the Merciless World

Love the Way Duet
Kiss Me
Hold Me
Love Me

With everything I've been through, and the unfortunate way we met, the last thing I thought I'd be focused on is the fact that I love the way you kiss me.

Extended epilogues to the Merciless World Novels
A Kiss To Keep (more of Sebastian and Chloe)
Seductive (more of Daniel and Addison)
Effortless (more of Carter and Aria)
Never to End (more of Seth and Laura)

Sexy, thrilling with a touch of dark Standalone Novels

Broken (Standalone)
Kade is ruthless and cold hearted in the criminal world.
They gave Olivia to him. To break. To do as he'd like.
All because she was in the wrong place at the wrong time. But there are secrets that change everything.
And once he has her, he's never letting her go.

Forget Me Not (Standalone novel)
She loved a boy a long time ago. He helped her

escape and she left him behind. Regret followed
her every day after.

Jay, the boy she used to know, came back, a man.

With a grip strong enough to keep her close and a
look in his eyes that warned her to never dare leave
him again.

It's dark and twisted.

But that doesn't make it any less of what it is.

A love story. Our love story.

<u>It's Our Secret</u> (Standalone novel)

It was only a little lie. That's how stories like these
get started.

But with every lie Allison tells, **Dean** sees
through it.

She didn't know what would happen. But with all
the secrets and lies, she never thought she'd fall for
him.

Small Town Romance

Tequila Rose Book 1

Autumn Night Whiskey Book 2

He tasted like tequila and the fake name I gave him
was Rose.

Four years ago, I decided to get over one man, by

getting under another. A single night and nothing more.

Now, with a three-year-old in tow, the man I still dream about is staring at me from across the street in the town I grew up in. I don't miss the flash of recognition, or the heat in his gaze.

The chemistry is still there, even after all these years.

I just hope the secrets and regrets don't destroy our second chance before it's even begun.

A Little Bit Dirty

Contemporary Romance Standalones

Knocking Boots (A Novel)

They were never meant to be together.
Charlie is a bartender with noncommittal tendencies.
Grace is looking for the opposite. Commitment. Marriage. A baby.

Promise Me (A Novel)
She gave him her heart. Back when she thought they'd always be together.

Now **Hunter** is home and he wants Violet back.

Tell Me To Stay (A Novella)

He devoured her, and she did the same to him.
Until it all fell apart and Sophie ran as far away
from **Madox** as she could.
After all, the two of them were never meant to be
together?

Second Chance (A Novella)

No one knows what happened the night that forced
them apart. No one can ever know.
But the moment **Nathan** locks his light blue eyes on
Harlow again, she is ruined.
She never stood a chance.

Burned Promises (A Novella)

Derek made her a promise. And then he broke it.
That's what happens with your first love.
But Emma didn't expect for Derek to fall back into
her life and for her to fall back into his bed.

You Are Mine Series of Duets

You Are My Reason (You Are Mine Duet book 1)
You Are My Hope (You Are Mine Duet book 2)

Mason and Jules emotionally gripping romantic
suspense duet.

One look and Jules was tempted; one taste,
addicted.

No one is perfect, but that's how it felt to be in
Mason's arms.

But will the sins of his past tear them apart?

You Know I Love You

You Know I Need You

Kat says goodbye to the one man she ever loved
even though **Evan** begs her to trust him.

With secrets she couldn't have possibly imagined,
Kat is torn between what's right and what was right
for them.

Tell Me You Want Me

This is Sue's story.

Valetti Crime Family Series:

A HOT mafia series to sink your teeth into.

Dirty Dom

Becca came to pay off a debt, but **Dominic Valetti**
wanted more.

So he did what he's always done, and took what he

wanted.

His Hostage
Elle finds herself in the wrong place at the wrong time. The mafia doesn't let witnesses simply walk away.
Regret has a name, and it's **Vincent Valetti**.

Rough Touch
Ava is looking for revenge at any cost so long as she can remember the girl she used to be.
But she doesn't expect **Kane** to show up and show her kindness that will break her.

Cuffed Kiss
Tommy Valetti is a thug, a mistake, and everything Tonya needs; the answers to numb the pain of her past.

Bad Boy
Anthony is the hitman for the Valetti familia, and damn good at what he does. They want men to talk, he makes them talk. They want men gone, bang - it's done. It's as simple as that.
Until Catherine.

Those Boys Are Trouble (Valetti Crime Family
Collection)

To Be Claimed Saga
A hot tempting series of fated love, lust-filled
secrets and the beginnings of an epic war.

Wounded Kiss
Gentle Scars

Collections of shorts and novellas

Don't Let Go
A collection of stories including:
Infatuation
Desires in the Night and Keeping Secrets
Bad Boy Next Door

Kisses and Wishes
A collection of holiday stories including:
One Holiday Wish
Collared for Christmas
Stolen Mistletoe Kisses

All I Want is a Kiss (A Holiday short)
Olivia thought fleeting weekends would be enough

and it always was, until the distance threatened to tear her and **Nicholas** apart for good.

Highest Bidder Series:

Bought

Sold

Owned

Given

From USA Today best selling authors, Willow Winters and Lauren Landish, comes a sexy and forbidden series of standalone romances.

Highest Bidder Collection (All four Highest Bidder Novels)

Bad Boy Standalones, cowritten with Lauren Landish:

Inked

Tempted

Mr. CEO

Three novels featuring sexy powerful heroes. Three romances that are just as swoon-worthy as they are tempting.

Simply Irresistible (A Bad Boy Collection)

Forsaken, (A Dark Romance cowritten with B. B. Hamel)
Grace is stolen and gifted to him; Geo a dominating, brutal and a cold hearted killer.
However, with each gentle touch and act of kindness that lures her closer to him, Grace is finding it impossible to remember why she should fight him.

View Willow's entire collection and full reading order at willowwinterswrites.com/reading-order

Happy reading and best wishes,
Willow xx

ABOUT W WINTERS

Thank you so much for reading my romances. I'm just a stay at home mom and avid reader turned author and I couldn't be happier.
I hope you love my books as much as I do!

More by W Winters
www.willowwinterswrites.com/books/

Sign up for my Newsletter to get all my romance releases, sales, sneak peeks and a **FREE** Romance, **Burned Promises**

If you prefer *text alerts* so you don't miss any of my new releases, text "Willow" to 797979

CONTACT W WINTERS
BOOKBUB | TWITTER | GOODREADS | EMAIL
INSTAGRAM | FACEBOOK PAGE | WEBSITE

Check out Wildflowers on Facebook - If I'm not
writing, I'm here!

CONNECT WITH AMELIA WILDE

Amelia Wilde is a USA TODAY bestselling author of dangerous contemporary romance and loves it a little *too* much. She lives in Michigan with her husband and daughters. She spends most of her time typing furiously on an iPad and appreciating the natural splendor of her home state from where she likes it best: inside.

Need more dangerous romance right now? Read her dark contemporary retelling of the famous Hades & Persephone right now in King of Shadows!

Need more stories like this one in your life? Sign up for her newsletter here and receive access to subscriber-only previews, giveaways, and more!

Follow her on BookBub for new release alerts!

Still can't get enough? Join her reader's group on Facebook and enter the party today!